To my sisters, Erin and Taylor. Though you may be near or far, I love you wherever you are.

Fall in love with each paw-fectly sweet adventure!

TABLE OF CONTENTS

Chapter 1
Relaxing to the Max

"Another mission in the doggie bag," said Noodles the labradoodle as she and the Love Puppy team hurried behind a large rosebush that grew in the corner of Leticia Smith's lawn.

"Yes!" said Rosie the golden retriever. "Job

well done, Pups!" Rosie swished her tail and each rosebud on the bush began to bloom. That was Rosie's specialty. She had magical flower power, which meant she could grow plants whenever and wherever she pleased.

As the leader of the Love Puppy team, Rosie looked warmly over each member of her squad. Clyde, the Shar-Pei, caught her eye as he took a celebratory flying flip and yipped, "We did it!" His magic gave him the ability to fly.

Rosie turned her gaze to Barkley, a miniature dachshund, who morphed into a purple pom-pom. Barkley's magic allowed him to transform into anything. Next, Rosie turned to Noodles, who then blew a gentle breeze to ruffle Barkley's shiny frill. Noodles had the ability to control elements of the weather.

This Love Puppy team spent their days helping kids in need and they enjoyed every moment of it. But their favorite part was always right after they successfully completed a mission. It meant another human child was helped out of a tough situation—just as Leticia had been!

So right then and there, each pup's jaws hung open in glee.

"That had to be a record," said Noodles, her big brown eyes shining. "We helped Leticia in the flick of a puppy's tail." She wiggled her tail with delight. "I think we earned a nice vacation."

"A *pup*-cation!" added Barkley. "Complete with umbrellas," he said, morphing his body into an umbrella and then into a lounge chair, "relaxation—"

"—and lots of snacks!" chimed in Clyde. He swooped in to rest on Lounge Chair-Barkley. Barkley changed back into his puppy body, and the two wrestled on the ground playfully.

"Let's head back and do it!" said Rosie. She held her paw out in front. Her paw pads began to glow pink. "Come on, Pups!"

All of the pups held out their paws, too, in the center of their puppy huddle. Each of their pads glowed like Rosie's: Noodles's orange, Clyde's blue, and Barkley's purple. "With the power of love—anything is possible. Love Puppies, go!"

As the magical portal known as the Doggie Door opened and the pups jumped through, off in the distance an anxious voice shouted: "Maxie! Maxie, come back!"

But the Love Puppies didn't hear the cry. Instead, with a *whoosh* and a flash of light and fur, the puppies transported from the human world back to the Doghouse—Love Puppy

Headquarters—and landed in their backyard. Their pup-cation started now!

Rosie padded across the yard toward her vegetable garden beside the house. The first-floor living room window overlooked her bountiful display of plants. Noodles's room had a garden view, too, but on the second floor.

"Hello, my beauties," Rosie said as her magic caused the plants to dance and wave to her. She was eager to give them some extra-tender love and care.

She used her teeth to grab her straw hat that hung on the wall and tossed it in the air. It fell right onto her head, her ears poking up through the Rosie-sized earholes. She stopped next to her blossoming tomato plant and inhaled deeply. "How about a nice drink?" she asked as she reached for the hose.

Meanwhile, Clyde flew through the air toward two large trees with a hammock strung between them. Balanced on his upturned paws, he held a tray of goodies he had grabbed from the kitchen. With a flying flip— and not one treat out of place—he landed on the hammock, tummy up. He placed the tray on his belly and called out: "Noodles—glasses me!"

Noodles, who was tanning beside the

bone-shaped pool, giggled and blew a huge gust of wind Clyde's way. This caused the sunglasses that were resting on the poolside table to take flight, tumble through the air, and land right on Clyde's eyes. Now the hammock rocked gently from the wind.

"Paw-fect!" Clyde said, swaying slightly before sipping from a pineapple. "Thank you, Noodles!"

"No problem, Clydie!"

"Cannonball!!!" shouted Barkley. He leapt high into the air and Noodles swept up another gust, helping Barkley propel toward the pool. Next, Barkley transformed from his puppy body into a giant purple ball and hit the water with a *SPLASH*. Noodles kicked up a wind, sending the splashing water flying in all directions—except for onto her own curly, dry fur.

"HEY!" called Clyde, now all soggy.

"Sorry about that." Noodles chuckled.

Clyde jumped down from the hammock, his snack tray already empty, and jetted toward the pool, taking a flying dive into the cool water. Each pup played and laughed, enjoying the warm, beautiful day.

As for Rosie, she continued watering her plants and snipping at stray growths in her garden. Suddenly, her ears perked up at a thumping sound. *TAP, TAP, TAP!*

"Hello?" Rosie looked around, trying to find the source of the sound.

Then, she noticed flashing coming from the living room window, followed by more tapping. She realized what it was—the Crystal Bone! It hovered near the living room window, buzzing and blinking.

The Crystal Bone was just as important to the team as each one of the puppies. Whenever a child was in need, it was the Crystal Bone that sounded the alarm. It would blink and buzz each time a new human was selected for help and a new mission began. But it was only Rosie who could receive the messages sent by the giant bone. She would place her paws on its smooth crystal surface and use her magic to get the information.

The way it blinked and buzzed at that moment told Rosie the pups were needed right away!

"Well," Rosie said to herself, "guess we'll have to relax later!"

So much for having it made in the shade!

Chapter 2
Mission Caleb

Rosie raced toward the swimming pool where all three of her Love Puppy teammates were swimming and splashing.

"Pups!" she called. "Pups! Someone needs our help! Out of the pool—we've got another mission!"

"I was just practicing my doggie paddle," said Clyde, kicking his strong legs beneath the water.

"I know, but we'll have to relax later. The Crystal Bone is flashing like wild!"

The other pups jumped out of the pool and shook the water from their fur. Noodles sent a warm wind over them, just to make sure they were good and dry.

As they hurried into the house, Clyde stopped by the bushes lining the house walls. "Does anyone else smell carrots?" he asked.

"You always smell food, silly pup," said Barkley. "It's just your tummy talking."

"Plus, you're probably just smelling Rosie's vegetable garden," said Noodles.

"Hmmm," Clyde said to himself, sniffing again. He was certain it smelled closer than the garden, which was located around the other side of the house. He shrugged his puppy shoulders. Maybe they were right—but a slice of carrot cake sure sounded delicious at that very moment.

"Come along, Pups!" Rosie urged.

The Crystal Bone met them by the door. It flashed and vibrated, levitating above the floor. The pups chased behind it as it zoomed into the living room and landed in its regular spot. The Love Puppy banner-pups pinned high on the wall yipped with anticipation.

Every banner included a moving picture of each of the puppies, and in their signature colors. These banners decorated the high walls of the Doghouse and certainly kept the pups entertained during downtimes.

But right now was anything but downtime. Rosie placed her paws on the Bone as she always did to get details about their latest mission. When her paws met the slick surface of its crystal, a profile and picture of a brown-haired boy projected onto the ceiling.

NAME: CALEB WRIGHT
Age: Seven
Grade: Second
Lost Pet: Maximus
Problem: Maximus ran away and Caleb cannot find him

"According to this, Maximus was last seen earlier today," Rosie explained.

Just then, the Bone projected a hologram of Caleb patting his pet tenderly. Caleb lifted Maximus into the air and then hugged him closely. Then the scene changed to Caleb playing with Maximus, feeding him, and jiggling a toy in front of him.

The pups watched as Maximus leapt from

Caleb's hands and dashed across the lawn and down the street with Caleb chasing behind, calling his name. Then Maximus ran out of sight and Caleb looked around frantically, crying out for him.

Noodles sucked in a big breath of air. Her nose began to tingle and she could feel tears puddling in her eyes. A gray cloud accumulated above her head, rumbling lightly with thunder and tiny sparks of lightning. She sniffed back the tears and closed her eyes.

Behind her eyelids, she pictured Pearla Ray, the tiny egg she had found in Rosie's garden that hatched into a caterpillar. Noodles had spent so much time with her little pet caterpillar, caring for her night and day, nurturing her and watching her grow. She still pictured Pearla's beautiful white, black, and yellow stripes inching across her paw.

But last month, Pearla wrapped herself into a cocoon, changed into a butterfly, and flew away. No matter how much Noodles had called to her, Pearla was gone for good.

Noodles opened her eyes again to see the last image of Caleb crying and calling out to Maximus. Noodles could feel Caleb's pain. The rain cloud above her head grew bigger and drops of rain began to fall on Noodles's fur.

Sadness felt like a heavy blanket in the room. Noodles hadn't realized it, but all the other pups' eyes fell on her.

"You all right, Noodles?" Rosie asked in a quiet tone.

Noodles nodded slowly. All of the puppies could still remember how hard their friend took the loss of Pearla Ray.

"We can do this mission without you, if you want," offered Clyde. He had scooched very close to Noodles and placed a paw around her shoulder.

Noodles sniffed some more, the tears finally finding their way down her fuzzy cheeks, mixing in with the wet from the rain cloud.

Noodles took a big breath and held it tight in her chest. She blew it out slowly and then took another breath. As she focused on her breathing, the rain cloud above her began to shrink until it was no longer there.

"That's okay," she finally said. "I definitely know how much it hurts to lose something you love," she whispered. "I want to help Caleb! If we can save him from a broken heart, I want to be a part of it."

"Okay," said Rosie. "Well, Pups, this is Mission Caleb. We have to help him find his pet . . ." Rosie stopped. "What is Maximus, anyway?"

Rosie placed her paws back on the Crystal Bone. An image of Maximus paused on the ceiling.

"Hmmm," said Rosie. "The Bone doesn't seem to know. But it did tell me Caleb calls him Maxie."

"Looks kind of like one of those guinea pigs to me," said Barkley.

"No, I think those are much smaller than Maxie," said Noodles.

"He is really fuzzy all over," said Rosie.

"Pups, I think it's a puppy. Caleb was even using puppy toys to play with him," said Clyde.

"That is true," said Noodles. "I think you

might be right, Clydie. But whatever it is, we've got to do our best to find Maxie and reunite him with Caleb!" Each of the puppies pictured little Maxie out there somewhere, lost and afraid.

"Caleb must be feeling so sad," said Clyde.

"Well, what are we waiting for? Let's go investigate at Caleb's house and find Maxie the puppy!" Noodles said, hopping onto her feet.

"Activating the Doggie Door portal," said Rosie, placing her paw in front of her. The other puppies joined in and they stated the magic words.

Whoosh!

Chapter 3
Missing Maxie

The pups landed in the backyard of a blue-painted house with a porch and a small grassy lawn. Large windows were open on each wall—so the pups were going to have to be extra careful not to be seen.

"Let's have a look around," whispered Rosie. "Maybe we can find which room is Caleb's."

"And if we're lucky," Noodles added, "maybe we can find Maxie, too." She and Rosie hurried to the left side of the house while Clyde and Barkley went to the right.

Noodles followed Rosie as she squeezed through the side gate and hurried to the front of the house. Rosie stopped in her puppy tracks, causing Noodles to bump right into her backside—*OOMPH!*

"Sorry about that," whispered Rosie as she helped Noodles to her feet. "It's just, this place feels kind of familiar."

"Yeah," Noodles added, "I thought so, too. Wait, isn't the house down there the one Leticia Smith lives in?" she asked, pointing her paw in the direction of a house way, way at the edge of the street.

"Oh yes! We *were* there on our last mission," replied Rosie. "That's strange! We've never helped two children who live so close to each other before."

"I guess there's a first time for everything. Come on, let's keep looking around."

Noodles placed her nose close to the ground and sniffed at the edge of the lawn. Then, she lifted her head and scanned the front yard before carefully checking from one edge to the other.

Rosie made her way to the porch. She looked under the chairs that rocked when she brushed against them. She even stuck her nose in each of the flowerpots, just to be sure. After both pups had covered every inch of the front yard, they met back up beside the porch.

"Anything?" asked Noodles.

"Nothing," responded Rosie. "Let's get back to the others."

This time, Noodles led the way from the front of the house, around the side, and then back to the backyard, where they found Barkley and Clyde huddling outside a window.

"Any luck finding Maxie?" asked Rosie in a hushed tone.

"Nope," replied Barkley, "but we found Caleb."

Just then, the soft sobs of a heartbroken boy drifted from the slightly open window.

Noodles and Rosie hurried over and looked in. Caleb lay on his bed, his face buried in his pillow. His body shuddered with sadness. Beside him, toys and treats were strewn across the top of his covers.

Noodles's nose tingled some more. She

shook her head, trying to relieve the sensation.
Then she returned her gaze to Caleb's room.
Right away, Noodles recognized the tiny red
squeezy ball. It was the same one the Bone
had shown Caleb and Maxie playing with.

The pups watched as Caleb's mother walked
into his room. She sat down beside him on the
bed and softly stroked his hair.

"I looked everywhere, Mom. I can't find him
anywhere."

"I know, love," she whispered. "And I know
you were so excited to show Maxie to your
cousins when they come visit next week. Maybe
we'll be able to find him by then. Don't give up

hope." She leaned over and kissed him on his head. "Come here," she said, "I want to show you something."

She led Caleb out of his bedroom, his head drooping low with grief.

"Poor, poor Caleb. What can we do?" asked Clyde.

"We already looked around the front yard and we couldn't see him anywhere," noted Rosie.

"And he's definitely not here in the backyard."

At that, Noodles's nose tingled again. She wiggled it and took a big sniff. "Maybe we didn't *see* Maxie anywhere—what about smell?! We pups have an expert sense of smell, right?"

All the pups nodded in agreement.

"But I don't know what Maxie smells like," added Clyde. None of the pups did.

Noodles looked back through the window. Caleb hadn't returned yet. Her eyes scanned the bed, where toys were laid all about.

"Aha! We can get one of his toys. It's bound to still have Maxie's smell on it! Yes, we need something of Maxie's to help us find him."

"Way ahead of you," said Barkley. The pups watched as he began to transform. His body shrank down and down as his feet stretched long like two flat paddles. His legs got longer, too, until he was a perfectly purple frog. "This should do the trick," he said. "Big enough to carry a toy but small enough not to be seen. I'm rrrrribbit-ready!"

"In that case," said Rosie with a chuckle, "hop to it!"

Barkley leapt onto the windowsill and into the bedroom. He jumped across the floor in the direction of Caleb's bed, in the center of the room. Noodles was right—Barkley could smell Maxie everywhere. And Caleb, too.

"Hurry, Barkley," whispered Noodles, "Caleb might be back at any moment."

Barkley frog-tailed it across the carpet as quickly as his little frog legs could carry him.

With a giant jump, he landed on the bed among Maxie's toys. He looked around—what would be a good pick?

"There!" he exclaimed. He shimmied over to the squeaky red ball and picked it up in his froggy mouth.

Suddenly, Caleb walked in and flopped down on the edge of the bed, causing Frog-Barkley to drop the ball and tumble toward him. Frog-Barkley landed two inches from Caleb's hand.

"Wait a minute," said Caleb as he looked down at the bed. "Where did you come from?"

The puppies held their breath. Had Barkley

been spotted? And would Caleb think this little purple frog might be the perfect replacement for a lost Maxie?

"Oh no!" whispered Noodles. "We've got to get him out of there!"

Chapter 4
A Close Call

Noodles's mind raced as she tried to think of what to do. It had been her idea to get one of Maxie's toys in the first place. So, it would be her fault if Caleb decided to keep Frog-Barkley for a pet. It would also be her fault if Barkley left a sad Caleb behind.

Noodles let out a giant sneeze caused by the tickle in her nose.

"Gesundheit," yipped Clyde. "Barkley told me that means 'Bless you!'"

"Thank you, Clydie," Noodles responded, with worry in her voice. Her eyes were still glued to Frog-Barkley.

But Caleb reached right past the purple frog-pup, who was lying super still on Caleb's bedsheets. Instead, he grabbed a blanket that had belonged to Maxie. He turned it over in his hands and spoke to himself under his breath about how his mom must have put it there. But as he held it, he looked at the blanket as if an idea was brewing in his mind.

"Any ideas about how we are going to get Barkley out of there," asked Clyde, "before Caleb spots him?"

As Noodles pondered what to do, Caleb shot up off the bed, still holding the blanket. "Mom! Mom! I think I know how to find Maxie!" he shouted as he raced from the room.

Noodles let out a big breath that she hadn't even realized she had been holding in. The other pups did, too.

"That was way too close," whispered Clyde.

"Come on, Barkley! You've got to get out of there before it's too late!"

Barkley bounced back to the ball and used his long, sticky tongue to grab it. As he hopped across the bed, he stopped on a slick piece of glass. He looked down at a framed picture of Caleb holding Maxie, smiling as brightly as the sun. Barkley looked back toward the door, then to the picture again.

"What's he doing?" whispered Rosie. "Get out of there, Barkley Boy."

Right there on the bed, Barkley morphed back into his puppy body.

"Barkley!" called Noodles.

The dachshund scooped up the ball with his paw and grabbed the picture with his teeth. With lightning speed, he jumped from the bed, dashed across the floor, and slipped through the open window just as Caleb returned to the room.

Back outside, and out of sight from Caleb, the pups jumped on Barkley, kissing his puppy face.

"That was too close," said Clyde.

"We were so scared," said Noodles, hugging Barkley tightly. "We thought we were going to lose you."

"Let's never do that again," said Rosie.

"I'm okay, Pups. I'm okay," responded

Barkley. "But look what I got—this," he said, holding up the ball with his paw, "and this." He lifted the picture of Maxie and Caleb together. "I'm pretty sure Maxie *is* a puppy, especially when you look at him here."

Maxie was a ball of fluff covering almost everything except his small black eyes. "He's one interesting-looking puppy! That's for sure," said Noodles.

"Yeah, like an extra-fluffy Pomeranian or something?" said Clyde.

"With those long droopy ears, maybe he's a basset hound," suggested Barkley.

"Whatever type of puppy he is, he sure is

cute," added Rosie. She ambled over to Barkley and licked his face. "These are great finds, Barkley Boy! They'll help us for sure!"

Then she turned back around to face the rest of her team. "So, Pups, we know what Maxie looks like. Now let's figure out what he smells like." She held up the ball. "Everybody, take a big whiff."

Each pup put their noses super close to the ball, inhaling deeply.

"He is an interesting-smelling puppy, too," said Clyde after sniffing, "but kind of familiar." The pups realized they could detect a little bit of Maxie's scent throughout the yard, now that they knew what he smelled like.

"Noodles, you go with Clyde. Barkley, you come with me. Let's find Maxie!" Rosie called. "Love Puppies, go!"

Once again, the Love Puppies split up, Maxie's scent fresh in their noses and their minds. Rosie and Barkley headed out into the neighborhood, keeping to the bushes while sniffing at every rock, tree, and mailbox they could find.

Noodles and Clyde took their place behind a big tree in Caleb's front yard.

"This should hide us," said Noodles.

"Hop on," urged Clyde.

It was clear Clyde already knew what she was thinking. Noodles climbed onto Clyde's back, and the two of them flew up through the branches of the tree.

"Since they're doing smell duty down there," called Clyde, "seems best if we take to the sky!" He broke through the branches at the very top of the giant tree and hovered just above them.

"This is good cover!" said Noodles. "No human should be able to see us up here."

Noodles and Clyde scanned the ground from their high-in-the-sky lookout. Noodles looked to the left—no Maxie. She looked to the right—no Maxie. She even lifted her nose to the clouds, sniffing deeply in hopes of picking up his scent.

"Do you see him?" asked Clyde.

"Nope. Don't smell him either. Do you?" she replied.

"That's a mastiff-sized no," said Clyde.

"Let's go back down and help the others."

When Clyde and Noodles landed on the ground, Barkley and Rosie were bounding toward them.

"Come here, Pups! Come here!" said Rosie. "We found his scent."

Noodles and Clyde took another whiff of the ball Rosie was holding.

"Now, follow me," Rosie said. The pups chased behind her.

Noodles's nose twinged. "I can smell him! I smell Maxie!" she said.

"Yes, but—" Before Rosie could finish her statement, Noodles blasted forward, tracing the Maxie scent down the block, past rows of homes and toward Leticia's house until—

"It's gone," Noodles said as the other pups finally caught up. "Maxie's scent was right here, but now I can't smell it anymore."

"Exactly," said Rosie, still catching her breath.

"That's what I was going to say. The scent ends here."

"We went farther around the corner and even into some of those other neighborhoods," said Barkley, pointing in different directions with his paws, "but it's no use. His scent just . . . stops."

"How can that be?" asked Noodles.

"We were asking that same question," said Rosie. "Maybe the sprinklers washed the smell away."

Noodles could see that the ground was wet, and her paws got a little soggy as they stood on the lawn.

"Maybe someone saw him and picked him

up. We are right here at the edge of the street," said Barkley.

"Would someone do that? Snatch up another person's lost puppy?" asked Noodles. That thought made each of the puppies feel even more worried.

"I don't know," answered Rosie. "But I don't think Maxie could have just vanished into thin air."

Each of the possibilities of what could have happened to Maxie left the pups feeling bluer and bluer. Even more worrisome was the fact that the sun was beginning to set, and it was getting late.

"Pups," started Rosie, "it's been a full day of Maxie hunting. We should head back home and rest. It'll give us a chance to sleep on it so we can think of what to do next."

With that, Rosie and the pups opened the portal.

But as Noodles jumped through it, her nose tingled again and she couldn't help but wonder: Would waiting a whole night make it impossible to *ever* find Maxie again?

Chapter 5
Rain Clouds and Butterflies

When the pups returned home, everyone was quiet. Their sad mood kept Noodles sneezing through dinner and bath time.

"Bless you, Noodles," said Rosie after another sneeze. "Are you getting sick?"

"I don't think so," responded Noodles, rubbing her nose. "Just a nose tickle."

"That's nothing that a good night's rest won't help," Rosie said, gently patting Noodles's fluffy cheek.

While that might be true, Noodles thought about how a good night's rest—actually, several, seeing as it had been over a month since Pearla Ray left—hadn't helped her feel better about *her* lost pet. No matter how many sleeps she had, her own heart still missed that striped caterpillar.

"Everything okay?" asked Barkley as he and Clyde padded into Noodles's room to say good night.

Noodles sighed a big sigh. "All this looking for Maxie is *really* making me miss my Pearla so much."

"Of course you miss her," said Rosie. "She was special to your heart."

"You took such good care of her, too," said Barkley.

"She was definitely the best-kept pet I had ever seen," added Clyde.

"It's okay if your heart hurts with missing her," Rosie said. "You might miss her for a little while or for a long, long time. But that's all right. That's what happens when you love something—if it is no longer there, then your heart will keep missing it."

"I bet that's just how Caleb feels," said Clyde. "His heart is missing Maxie."

"If I ever lost one of you, my heart would miss *you* forever!" said Barkley.

"That's how I felt today when you almost got caught, Barkley," said Noodles. "I would have been sad forever and ever and ever!"

"Me too!" they all agreed. By now, all the pups were nestled beside Noodles in a puppy-hug-huddle.

"It takes time for your heart to heal when a loved one is no longer there," Rosie said once more. "But if you ever need to just talk about how you are feeling, that's what we're here for!"

"Thanks, Pups," Noodles said. She kissed each of their cheeks and told them good night as they headed to their own rooms.

Noodles walked over to the wall next to her window. Pictures of Pearla that she had drawn and colored were taped there. One was a sketch of Pearla as a tiny white egg before she hatched. Noodles remembered how much time she spent getting each detail just right on Pearla's egg.

She looked over the other pictures: Pearla inching across her paw. Pearla munching on leaves. Even the time Pearla was a butterfly, flittering on Noodles's nose—before she flew away and never came back. And then the many pictures a heartbroken Noodles had drawn of Pearla in her beautiful butterfly form.

Sharing her feelings with the pups had made her feel a little better, although her heart still ached.

She ran her eyes over a letter she had written Pearla when she felt really low. A letter that Typewriter-Barkley had helped her write, even though she knew Pearla would never get it. Still, it had felt nice to write. She read over the words again:

Dear Pearla,

Hi. I miss you so much. I know
you are a beautiful butterfly
now. You are probably exploring
the big, wide world out there.
Touching the clouds and the sky.
Sipping from pretty flowers. I still
wish you would come back to me.
It's okay if you don't. Just know
I love you and miss you so, so
much.

Love,
Noodles

Noodles had even signed the letter with her

paw-print.

She trotted over to her doggie-bed. Maxie's

toy ball and the picture of Maxie and Caleb

were on top of her blanket. She picked up

the ball and picture and closed her eyes.

She couldn't help the tears or the drizzle from the rain cloud above her head. The drops rinsed over her and the items until she took more deep breaths, calmed her sad, and blew it away with each exhale. Taking deep breaths often helped her quiet her feelings.

She looked down at Caleb's and Maxie's things again and took a sniff.

"Wait a minute," she said to herself. She took another sniff. "Oh no! I can't smell Maxie anymore." She lifted the ball all the way up to her nose and smelled some more. No matter how she sniffed, his scent was gone. Washed away by her tears and her cloud's sadness downpour.

How were they ever going to find him now that she had accidentally erased his smell?

Chapter 6
Shelter from the Storm

Noodles tossed and turned all night. Thoughts swirled through her puppy brain. A scared Maxie. A sad Caleb. A lost Pearla.

She hugged both Maxie's ball and the picture of Maxie and Caleb to her chest.

She sniffed at Maxie's ball again just to double-check—nothing!

Noodles climbed out of her bed and headed to her window. She opened it to let the cool air roll over her fur. She still held Caleb's things as she looked out at Rosie's garden and up at the night moon. Something rustled right outside the window—woodland creatures out at night, no doubt. Maybe an owl or a hedgehog?

"Nocturnal animals don't sleep at night," she said to herself. "I guess I'm nocturnal now."

Noodles hugged the items once more. Her heart picked up. She pulled the ball close to her nose again. She could pick up the faint smell of Maxie. What a relief! She hadn't completely washed it away.

"I'd better put these somewhere, so I don't mess them up again," she said. She carefully placed the picture and the toy on the windowsill.

Feeling a little less worried, she climbed back in bed and finally tumbled into sleep.

* * *

The next morning, a groggy Noodles padded into the living room.

"Rise and shine, pretty pup," said Rosie. Noodles grabbed a bowl of kibble and joined the rest of the pups as they ate their breakfasts from their own bowls.

"So, what's our next move?" asked Barkley.

"Good question," responded Rosie. "Sniffing for Maxie's scent only took us so far."

"And we definitely didn't spot him when we took to the sky," said Clyde, between bites of breakfast.

"But what about someone scooping him up?" added Noodles. "Do you think if someone spotted him, maybe they would have taken him to a lost pet home?"

"Oh, like a shelter!" added Rosie. "That's a great idea—and it sounds like our next move.

Check out the shelters that are near Caleb's house."

After the pups finished their meal, Rosie hurried over to the Crystal Bone to do a quick check of the shelters that were close to Caleb's home.

"We've got three to check out," she said right before they opened the Doggie Door and she led her friends through the portal. "Tender Heart Sanctuary, Safe Pets R Us, and A Home for Pets. First up: Tender Heart Sanctuary. With the power of love—anything is possible. Love Puppies, go!"

Whoosh!

Tender Heart Sanctuary was a tiny building with large windows and a big, red front door. The pups hid behind a hedge that bordered the building.

"It looks just like a house," said Clyde.

"Are you ready, Barkley?" asked Noodles. Her heartbeat sped up as she thought about what happened the last time. "You've just got to be careful. And don't get spotted."

Barkley chuckled and said, "This will be a . . ." and morphed his body into a purple piece of chocolate cake. He giggled, but when he remembered what their mission was, he focused on the task ahead and transformed into a ladybug.

"Look at the picture again, Barkley," said Rosie, holding up the photo of Caleb and Maxie. "This is what you are looking for."

"Got it," said Ladybug-Barkley. He fluttered through the window.

"Don't worry," said Rosie to Noodles, "he'll be fine."

But shortly after he left, he returned with bad news: "No sign of him anywhere," said Barkley, back in his pup body.

The same went for Safe Pets R Us and A Home for Pets.

"This mission is seeming just about as im-paw-sible as can be!" said Rosie. "Maybe

63

we should check in on Caleb to see if he has any news."

When the pups got to Caleb's house and looked in through his window, they found him busy at work.

"What's he doing?" asked Clyde.

Caleb grabbed a piece of paper with a picture of Maxie on it. Then he wrote the word *Missing* on the top in big red letters and a phone number on the bottom.

"He's making signs!" Noodles said. "Great idea, Caleb!" It was nice to see that the boy had dried his tears and was working hard to find his Maxie. "We can help him! We're excellent at posting signs," she said with excitement in her yip.

As soon as Caleb stepped out of the room, they put their plan into motion. Noodles pushed the window open a little wider.

"Let it rip!" she said before taking a huge breath and sending a tornado wind whipping through Caleb's room. The tornado swept up the sheets of paper and the tape dispenser and twirled them toward the window, out into the backyard, and stacked them neatly into a pile at the puppies' feet.

"Nicely done, Noodles!" said Barkley.

"Wait, won't Caleb realize they are missing?" asked Clyde.

"Maybe. But I'm sure once he steps outside and sees them already posted, he will be as happy as a puppy at the park," said Noodles.

She was just glad they didn't have to send Barkley back inside Caleb's room.

"Let's go!" said Noodles.

Off the pups raced to post the signs all over the neighborhood without anyone noticing them. It ended up being as easy as they thought it would be. Barkley passed a page to Rosie, who added the tape. She passed the sign to Noodles, who blew it up in the air to Clyde, who posted it in the perfect spot.

In less than an hour, signs plastered Caleb's neighborhood and a few of the blocks nearby.

Back outside Caleb's window, Rosie said, "Now we wait."

And wait and wait.

By lunchtime, there still had been no calls for Caleb.

The pups watched him as he pulled clothes from his drawers, upturned his bedsheets, and reached under his bed.

"What's Caleb up to now?" asked Clyde as he eyed Caleb hurrying around the bedroom.

"I don't know what happened to them," he shouted to his mom. "They were right here."

"Maybe we can make some more," said his mom, who now stood at the door watching Caleb search and search.

"But that was the last of my allowance. I used it to make the copies of the signs. And to get the markers and tape."

"I'm sure I can help you with it this time," said his mother.

"Uh-oh," added Rosie, watching Caleb and his mother closely. "Maybe us posting the papers didn't help at all."

"Now he thinks they're lost," said Barkley. "If only he'd just go outside."

"Forget it," said Caleb, falling back onto

his bed. "I really tried everything to get him back. I don't know what else to do."

Caleb's mom sat beside him on the bed and put her arm around him. It was clear he wouldn't be going outside anytime today.

"It doesn't matter anymore," said Caleb in a quiet voice. "Maxie is long gone by now. He's never coming back."

Noodles's nose twitched again. She was out of ideas, too. And she was sure the other pups were as well.

"Pups," whispered Noodles, sniffing sadly. "I think Maxie might actually be gone forever."

"Well," said Rosie solemnly, "that means our mission shifts from finding Maxie to helping Caleb cope with the loss of his loving pup."

Those were some of the saddest words Noodles had ever heard.

Chapter 7
Garden Gone

The Love Puppies transported back to headquarters for lunch and to do some more brainstorming.

That was the perfect description, too: brainstorming. Because Noodles sat in a rain puddle as her thundercloud rumbled and lightning flashed over her head.

Why had they failed Caleb in such a big way? How is it that they used their best powers and *still* came up empty-pawed?

Truly, the Love Puppies had tried their hardest to find Maxie. They searched neighborhoods and shelters. They looked high and low. They posted lost signs and sniffed for Maxie's scent. But he was still gone.

If Maxie really was gone forever, there wasn't anything even a magical puppy could do to bring him back.

Rosie looked over her team of pups as they

huddled on the living room floor. Each one looked so very sad.

"Tell you what, Pups," she said, "I'll make my famous vegetable and bone soup. That should cheer us up at least a little."

"You do make a pup-tastic soup!" said Clyde, way less peppy than usual. "Maybe that's just what we need—full bellies to chase away the blues."

"We can eat while we decide what to do next," added Rosie. She headed out to the garden to gather vegetables.

"I'll go grab Maxie's toy and picture again," said Noodles. "Maybe those things can help us think of how to help Caleb. I'll be right back!"

Noodles bounded toward her room. As she approached the open window, she could tell instantly that something was off. The picture was still on the windowsill, but the ball was gone.

"Where did Maxie's ball go?" She searched around her room, looking on the floor and under her bed. She searched the closet and every other corner and nook of her room. It was nowhere to be found.

"Pups!" Rosie's voice called from down the hallway. "My vegetable garden! Some of my crops are missing."

"Wasn't me," answered Clyde. He and the other pups joined Rosie at the front door.

"I also can't find Maxie's ball," Noodles said with a quiet voice.

First Pearla, then Maxie, the ball, and Rosie's vegetables—what else was going to go missing!

"I worked really hard on those vegetables," said Rosie.

"They were going to be delicious," added Clyde.

Rosie looked in Noodles's direction. "It does really hurt to lose something you care about. At least *my* lost things were just some vegetables I can grow more of."

Noodles nodded in agreement. "Can you imagine how Caleb is feeling about Maxie?"

"Or you about Pearla," added Barkley. "What do you do to make yourself feel better, Noodles?"

Noodles sighed deeply. "Well, sometimes I don't feel better at all. Other times, I feel okay. It comes kind of like waves in our swimming pool: one day okay, another day not."

And just like Rosie had said, Noodles knew that was okay.

"But talking to you pups about it really helps me," added Noodles.

"I remember right after Pearla left, you also

did some creative things to show your love," said Rosie. "Didn't you draw pictures?"

"Oh yeah! And you wrote her a letter!" said Clyde. "I saw it hanging on your bedroom wall. Did those things help?"

Noodles smiled and nodded. "They did help! So did the books you shared, Rosie. The ones about saying goodbye."

"Those are some of my favorite books to read when I feel sad," said Rosie. "Maybe we can read some of those books again together at bedtime."

"I also really like hugging things that remind me of Pearla. Like her favorite toy leaf. But," continued Noodles, "hugging you pups helps me feel best of all!"

With that, the Love Puppies dashed toward Noodles, burying her in a puppy pileup.

"I bet some of these ideas can help Caleb feel better about losing Maxie, too," said Rosie.

"Yeah," said Noodles, who was on the bottom of the pile, "because even when the sad feelings come back and I miss my Pearla, doing all these things again helps me feel better. Pups," she added with a tail wag, "I think we've got our next plan to help Caleb. Let's get to work!"

Chapter 8
A Moment of Goodbye

Back outside Caleb's window, the pups stood in a circle.

"Okay, so we all decided talking to someone you love about your sad feelings can help. Maybe we can start with that," said Noodles.

"Caleb was looking forward to showing Maxie off to his cousins," said Rosie. "Maybe he'd want to talk to them about how he feels?"

"But they're not coming to visit until next week," said Clyde.

Noodles smiled. "That doesn't mean Caleb can't talk to them now, when he really needs their support."

"But what do humans use to talk with each other?" asked Barkley.

"Their mouths?" added Clyde. "Or their hands."

"Of course, silly pup," says Rosie with a

giggle. "I mean, is there something else they can use to talk?"

"Or maybe some*one* else he could talk to," said Barkley. "Like his mom."

"That could work. But how would we bring them together?" asked Rosie. "I don't want to send you back in there, Barkley—last time you came way too close to never coming back out! And there's no way we could do that without getting caught."

"Plus, he talks to his mom all the time," said Noodles.

Barkley's shoulders sagged. "I guess Caleb

will have to figure that one out on his own."

"What about things he can use to draw or write?" said Clyde. "Like how Noodles made pretty pictures of Pearla."

"Now, *that's* a good idea!" said Rosie. "Plus, Caleb already has a bunch of supplies there on his desk. Maybe we can move them to his bed to remind him."

With perfectly placed wind gusts, Noodles lifted paper, markers, pens, and pencils onto Caleb's bed.

"Paw-fect! We'll wait for him to come in and see them," said Rosie.

Caleb walked in holding a shoebox. His eyes

were still puffy and red. It was clear he had been crying again.

He stopped and looked at his desk before walking over to it. He picked up a water dish, pellet bowl, and some small plastic toys and placed them on top of the shoebox lid. Then he lifted the tiny blanket from before and held it to his heart.

Caleb carried all these items over to his bed and sat on the floor next to it. But the bed blocked the puppies' view.

"What's he doing?" asked Clyde. "I can't see him. Even when I fly up high."

"I don't know," said Barkley, "but he still

hasn't noticed the supplies on the bed."

Caleb ducked down so they could no longer see his brown hair poking up from the other side of the bed. He stood up again and walked to another corner of his bedroom, lifting a large cage and leaving the room with it in his arms.

"What was that all about?" asked Clyde.

"Not sure," said Rosie, "but I'm running out of ideas of what to do to help. I thought maybe I could get the book I read to help me feel less sad and place it on his bed. But if he didn't even see the supplies, I don't think he'd see the book either."

"Unless . . ." added Noodles. "Let's open the Doggie Door portal. I have another idea!"

The pups opened the portal just big enough for Noodles to jump through.

"I know what to do to help Caleb see the supplies. I'll be right back!"

* * *

Once she was through the portal, Noodles dashed full speed toward her room.

Maybe she had made a few mistakes on this mission—like her idea of taking Caleb's posters to hang up or losing Maxie's favorite toy—but she was determined to make it all right. It was clear Maxie wasn't coming back.

But that didn't mean the pups couldn't still help.

"Aha!" she said, spotting the picture on the windowsill. This would do the trick.

Placing the picture of Maxie and Caleb on the bed next to the art supplies was sure to catch his attention. Caleb would see the picture, remember the wonderful times he had with Maxie, and capture his feelings on the materials the pups had supplied.

This *had* to work. Because if it didn't, Noodles had no other ideas.

Noodles snapped the picture up in her jaws and headed back through the portal to the human world. When she returned, all of the pups were on their hind legs, paws pressed up against the window and tails wagging excitedly.

"Look, Noodles!" said Rosie.

Noodles hurried over to the window, picture frame still between her teeth

Through the window, Noodles could see Caleb. He was holding the markers they had placed on his bed. But he wasn't drawing or making a picture with them. Instead, he was writing words on one of the sheets of paper the pups had put there.

"I think he's writing a letter," said Rosie.

"Just like you did for Pearla," said Barkley.

Their supplies had worked!

Caleb picked up the sheet and stared at it. Then he smiled a small smile as a tear rolled down his cheek.

Wait! He was still sad? Maybe it didn't work after all.

Caleb's mother stepped into the room. "Are you ready?" she asked. She wore a lovely black dress with black shoes.

"Almost," said Caleb. Noodles then realized he was dressed in black pants and a smooth white shirt. "I just can't find his favorite ball. It's red and squishy. I can't find it anywhere."

"That's okay. You have his other things, right?" asked his mother.

Caleb nodded and kneeled down next to the bed. He pulled out the box he held earlier. He grabbed one of the markers and wrote "I love you" on the top of the lid and hugged the box closely to his chest.

He reached for the letter on the bed. "Okay, I'm ready." He and his mother left the room with him holding the box and letter.

The pups watched from around the corner, hidden by the bushes and the wall. Caleb and his family—all dressed in black and white, his father holding a small bouquet of flowers—walked outside to the backyard. They stopped at a table in the center of the lawn.

Caleb opened the box he held and laid out Maxie's things on the table: the plastic toys, the water and food dishes, the blanket, and other items. He placed them with care next to the cage he must have put there earlier.

The family stood in a circle around the table.

"Would you like to start?" Caleb's mother asked, looking in his direction.

Caleb shook his head. His eyes stared down at his own feet.

"I can begin if you like," she said.

Caleb nodded.

"Maxie was such a special guy. He filled our lives with so much joy and he will be sorely missed." Caleb's father handed his mother a flower. She carefully placed it in the box.

Next, Caleb's sister said some words and placed her flower, followed by his little brother and then his father.

"Are you ready now, love?" said his mother in a soft tone.

Caleb wiped his eyes and unfolded his letter. In a tiny voice, he began: "Maxie, I am so sad you are gone. I miss you every day. You were my best friend. I hope you are happy. I hope you are okay. I hope you come home.

But if you don't, I will still love you forever."

As Caleb folded up the letter, his father walked over and hugged him. He handed him a flower. Caleb placed both the letter and the flower into the shoebox.

The family held hands and all together said, "Goodbye, Maxie."

Caleb added, "We love you."

Noodles's nose tingled like tiny ants were dancing all over it. But no rain cloud came.

Noodles also saw that even though the family had tears in their eyes and on their cheeks, their faces didn't only look sad. A little hint of contentment was there, like thinking about better times. Each face seemed to hold so much love. Maybe for Maxie, but also for one another.

After that, Noodles knew in her heart that Caleb was going to be okay.

"Let's go get something to eat," said Caleb's father. The pups watched as the family went back into the house. They could hear the car start outside and the tires pull away and drive off.

But the pups stood statue-still in their spots, huddled next to one another. Noodles's nose tickled so much that she thought she would . . .

"AAAAACHOOOOO!" she blew.

"Bless you," said Rosie.

Noodles shook her head and then leaned

down to pick up the framed picture of Maxie and Caleb. As she lifted it, the world seemed a little brighter to her. She wasn't sure why, but she liked it.

Noodles slowly walked toward the table. She stood on her hind legs, grasping the table's edge with her paws. Gently, she stood the framed picture up and used her nose to gently nudge it next to Maxie's items on the table.

"Goodbye, Maxie. And goodbye, Pearla," she whispered. She turned back to her team of pups.

With the sight of her, the puppies gasped.

"Noodles," said Rosie, "your nose!"

"Huh?" she replied.

What used to be a tiny brown labradoodle nose was now an orange, heart-shaped nose. At this moment, her nose glowed bright orange, just like her paw pads did when she activated her magic. The light shed a beautiful hue over the yard and the puppies.

This mission had been different for the pups. It had been a tough one. It had changed them.

Even though Noodles's heart still felt the sadness of losing Pearla, she felt a lightness about her. Maybe *she* was going to be okay, too.

"Come on, Pups," she said. "Let's go home."

Chapter 9
Pearla Ray Blues

Back at the Doghouse, the beautiful moment shared with Caleb's family was still fresh in each of the pups' minds. As was the new and bright nose that adorned Noodles's face.

"That was really special," said Rosie, sitting

on the puppy lounge in the living room. She and all the other pups had just finished their dinner and baths. "I had never seen something like that before."

"It was," added Barkley. "But we've also never failed a mission before today."

"I don't think we failed," said Noodles. "We learned a really valuable lesson about how to say goodbye when we lose someone or something we love."

"That's true," said Clyde. "Hey, why don't we hold a Moment of Goodbye for Pearla—like Caleb and his family did for Maxie!"

"We can do it in the garden, where there are

beautiful flowers all around!" added Rosie.

Noodles's nose lit up with excitement from that thought. "YES! I love that idea."

All of the puppies padded through the house and out the front doggie door and into the garden. They stood in a circle, just as they had seen the humans do.

"I can go first, Noodles," said Rosie. "If you like?"

Noodles nodded her furry head.

"I remember one time when Pearla, Noodles, and I all went out into my garden," began Rosie. "We put Pearla on a pile of leaves, and she gobbled them up like it was the tastiest meal she had ever eaten. I'll miss you, pretty caterpillar *and* butterfly."

"Thank you," said Noodles.

"Pearla was a good eater," said Clyde as he started his speech. "She was a bug after my own heart. I hope she's eating as much—wait, what do butterflies eat?" asked Clyde, looking at Noodles.

"Sweet nectar from flowers, I suppose," said Noodles.

"Mmmm, nectar," said Clyde. "I hope she's eating nectar until her big butterfly belly is nice and full."

"Thank you, Clydie," said Noodles.

"Pearla Ray," said Barkley, "I hope you are flying as high as the stars. We'll miss you for as long as we can."

Next it was Noodles's turn.

"I didn't tell you guys this, but I actually wrote a song for Pearla. Here it goes." She cleared her throat, took a deep breath, and sang:

"Pearla Ray, my Pearla Ray.
I miss you every single day.
I find myself so down and blue
Each moment I'm away from you.
And though you may be near or far
I love you wherever you are.
Although I may feel down and blue,
I love you, love you, love you."

The puppies joined in with soft howls and yips.

"Goodbye, Pearla Ray," said Noodles.

"Goodbye, Pearla—" But just as the pups began to repeat Noodles's words, they heard a crash from beneath Noodles's bedroom window.

Without a moment to think, Noodles blew a fierce wind in the direction of the bushes, where the sound came from.

Out from the bushes flew a red ball and—

"MAXIE!!!" shouted the pups.

"It's really him! It's Maxie! He's here!"

"How?" asked Rosie. But none of the pups

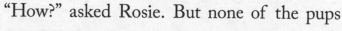

answered. They were too busy dashing in the direction of the real-life Maxie.

"I can't believe it! We've found him!" called Noodles, her nose shining like a star. "We found Maxie!"

"Actually, Maxie found us," said Clyde.

Either way, how? How could that be?

Chapter 10
Maxie Comes Back

The pups crowded around the bush where Maxie had hurried to hide.

"Why's he so scared?" asked Clyde. "We're nice pups. We aren't going to bite him."

"Well, I think if a bunch of doggies that you

didn't know came running at you, you'd probably feel a little scared, too," answered Noodles.

"How do we get that silly pup out of there?" asked Barkley.

"I'm still trying to figure out how he got here in the first place," said Rosie. Her mind was racing with so many questions of how, how, *how*! No one from the human world had ever come to the Doghouse before.

Clyde knelt down and sniffed beneath the bush. "Yep, that's Maxie for sure. I remember his scent from the ball. But he smells like something else, too." He sniffed at Maxie's fluffy tail. "Carrots, I think."

"Carrots? Wait," started Barkley, "didn't you say something smelled like carrots the other day? And we said it was probably Rosie's garden?"

Clyde nodded.

"That was the same day I heard something thumping outside," Noodles said, motioning to her open window right above them, "when I couldn't sleep."

"We've also got the missing ball. Maxie was the toy snatcher," said Rosie. "And the garden vegetable thief." Rosie motioned to bits of half-eaten carrots and carrot tops poking out from under the bush.

That still didn't answer the question of *how*.

"Hold on," said Noodles. All these clues showed that Maxie had been here all along, since early in their Caleb Mission. "You sneaky puppy! I know how he got here. He must have leapt through the Doggie Door portal when we finished Mission Leticia!"

"Oh yes! We did say we smelled his scent all the way up to Leticia's house," said Barkley, "and then it vanished."

"Exactly. That would explain why we couldn't find him in the human world. He was in the Love Puppy universe all along!" exclaimed Rosie.

"Uh, Pups," said Clyde, still kneeling down trying to inspect Maxie. "Do puppies have fuzzy tails that look like cotton? Or long ears that don't always droop?"

"What are you talking about, Clydie?" asked Rosie.

Finally, Clyde sat up. "I don't think Maxie's a puppy. I think he's a—"

"—a bunny rabbit!" interjected Noodles.

"I was going to say giant hamster," said Clyde, "but I like your guess better."

"It all makes so much sense now. Caleb's Maxie is a bunny rabbit. The flash of our portal must have startled him and caused him to flee. Right through the Doggie Door—whoosh!"

"If he's a bunny rabbit, I know just how to get him out of there!" Barkley said. He shrank down, down, down into a carrot. "Come on out, little guy!"

Just as Maxie opened his mouth for a bite, Barkley transformed into his puppy body and hugged him gently.

"Let's get this little guy home!" said Noodles, her nose glowing with the warm light of love.

Chapter 11
Hearts That Heal

Under the dim light, sprawled out on the living room carpet, the Love Puppies sat all together, staring up at the ceiling.

"Again, Bone," said Noodles.

Projected onto the ceiling was a hologram of

Noodles, carefully placing Maxie onto Caleb's bed and then hurrying back out the window.

Then, Caleb came into the room, stopping mid-step in shock before running over to his once-lost bunny. Caleb picked up Maxie, held him close, and kissed his bunny mane.

"Where did you come from?" he whispered into Maxie's fur. Caleb looked toward his open window where the pups were huddled right out of sight.

"It doesn't matter. You're home, you're home! I missed you, Maxie-Max!" Caleb ran into the hallway, his voice echoing off the walls. "Mom!" he called. "Mom, you're not going to believe it. It's him! He's back! Maxie's back!"

The hologram paused with Caleb's empty bedroom in view.

"What a mission this one was, right, Pups?" said Rosie.

"So much to take from it," added Noodles.

"Like making sure there are no other animals around when we open the portal," said Clyde.

"So true," chuckled Rosie. "But also, when we lose someone we love, there are things we can do to help ourselves feel better. Even if we are sad for a long time."

"Yeah, like telling your friends and family how you are feeling," added Barkley.

"Or doing something creative," said Noodles, "like drawing a picture, writing a letter—"

"Or singing a beautiful song, like the 'Pearla Ray Blues,'" said Rosie.

"You can also read books about saying goodbye," said Clyde, "or say some really pretty words with others about the loved one you lost. Oh, chicken submarine sandwich, how I miss you."

"Yes, but most important of all," added Noodles, her nose beginning to glow, "sometimes, you may have to just let your heart hurt until it is ready to heal—which may take a long time. And that's okay. Eventually, you might feel better, but even when the sad comes back—that's okay, too."

"Sometimes lost things can come back, like Maxie," said Clyde. "But other times, they don't."

"Like Pearla Ray," said Noodles.

Rosie added, "Saying goodbye is really hard, but it can also show how much love you have."

"Yes. And there will always be times we have to let go and move on in search of brighter days. Moving on isn't easy, but we have to do it. It's just a part of life." Noodles smiled and eyed Maxie's toy—a reminder of this mission that she decided to keep.

She knew that in time, she'd be okay and ready to move on. But for now, she hummed the "Pearla Ray Blues" to herself.

"You know what?" began Clyde. "Our successful mission calls for a celebration!"

"What do you have in mind?" asked Noodles.

"Carrot cake, anyone?" said Clyde. "With extra bacon bits?"

Well, that was a magical idea that would brighten anybody's blue day.

Want more Love Puppy magic?

Read on for a sneak peek at their next adventure!

Chapter 1
Puppy Play

"Hup, hup! Go looooooong!" shouted Barkley just before he took flight.

Barkley was no regular dachshund puppy—he was one of the magical Love Puppies. And his special skill was transformation, which he had used to turn himself into a purple Frisbee. His friend Rosie, a golden retriever, was currently holding him gently between her teeth. With a flick of her head, Rosie let go of Frisbee-Barkley and he flew through the air.

"Send him my way, Noodles!" called Clyde the Shar-Pei. Noodles, a labradoodle, used her magic to whip up a wind. Frisbee-Barkley twirled and floated right up to Clyde, who used his power of flight to soar up into the sky and catch the purple Frisbee with his paws. With a flying flip, Clyde landed on the ground, Frisbee-Barkley in tow.

"Now that was un-Fris-bee-lievable!" called Clyde with a yip.

Rosie grinned and activated her own flower magic, sending a shower of petals dancing over her Love Puppy team. Each of the puppies giggled and nipped at the twirling petals. Then they fell into a doggie pile, overcome with joyful laughter.

"What should we do now, Pups?" asked Rosie. The pups rested under the warm sun in the backyard of their Love Puppy Headquarters. Rosie laid on the top of the pile, belly up.

"We could play a game of 'What's That Smell?'" said Clyde.

"Nah," said Barkley as he transformed back in his regular body. "With Noodles's new nose, she could smell almost anything from ten miles away."

It was true. After one particular Love Puppy mission, Noodles's nose had changed into the shape of a heart and glowed whenever she felt strong emotions. It also heightened her ability to smell and helped her to know if someone was in need.

And Rosie, who was the leader of the puppies, had gained a new talent, too. A heart on her chest glowed vibrantly to alert her to children who needed the Love Puppies' special brand of help. It also let her keep an eye on friends they helped in the past. All she had to do was activate the glowing heart and it allowed for her to check in on those friends, just like a window into their lives. So far, all the humans they had assisted in previous missions were doing very well.

As for Clyde and Barkley, they hadn't developed any new powers. Yes, Clyde could fly and Barkley could transform into just about anything. Not to mention when they combined their powers with Noodles and Rosie, they could open the Doggie Door portal, giving them entrance to the human world.

But other than that—no new superpowers for those two.

"How about we eat a nice tuna fish sandwich?" asked Clyde.

"We just ate lunch, silly pup," responded Rosie.

"Did we?" said Clyde. The giant bowl of Bones and Bits he had just finished up had clearly slipped his mind.

"Well, maybe we could—" began Barkley, but he stopped mid-sentence. Right at that moment, Noodles's nose glowed bright orange and Rosie's chest heart illuminated pink.

"Guess we won't be needing something to do," said Rosie, jumping to her feet. "Looks like we've got a new mission. Come on, Pups! Let's head inside."

They knew that the Crystal Bone would be flashing and vibrating with urgent news of the next mission. All the puppies jumped right up and chased after Rosie.

Except for Barkley. He hadn't moved. He stayed back for a moment more, scratching at his ear with his hind leg.

Usually, new missions got Barkley so excited. But even with the possibilities of this new adventure, Barkley could not help but wonder if he'd ever get a new gift like Rosie and Noodles had.